WANTED!

KATE THOMPSON

Illustrated by Jonny Duddle

RED FOX

WANTED!

A RED FOX BOOK 978 1 862 30519 9

First published in Great Britain by The Bodley Head,
an imprint of Random House Children's Publishers UK
A Random House Group Company

The Bodley Head edition published 2010
This edition published 2012

1 3 5 7 9 10 8 6 4 2

Typeset in Caslon Antique 16.3/22pt

RANDOM HOUSE CHILDREN'S PUBLISHERS UK
61–63 Uxbridge Road, London W5 5SA

www.**kids**at**randomhouse**.co.uk
www.**totallyrandombooks**.co.uk
www.**randomhouse**.co.uk

Addresses for companies within The Random House Group Limited can
be found at: www.**randomhouse**.co.uk/offices.htm

THE RANDOM HOUSE GROUP Limited Reg. No. 954009

A CIP catalogue record for this book is available from the British Library.

Printed and bound in Great Britain by CPI Group (UK) Ltd,
Croydon, CR0 4YY

CHAPTER ONE

It was early afternoon on a cold February day. I had just finished my deliveries and was making my way home across the city with my handcart. The streets were quiet, as they usually were at that time of day, so I had no trouble hearing the horse when it came trotting up behind me, and I moved aside with my cart to let it pass.

But it didn't. The young man who was leading it stopped beside me, and when I turned to look at him I was astonished by what I saw. He was a slave, and I might have been struck by how well-dressed he was if I hadn't noticed that the horse was dressed even better. It wore a blanket of royal purple and its head collar was decorated with precious stones which sparkled in rainbow colours. Its lead rope was a chain of solid gold. I stood with my mouth open, astonished. I ought to have known immediately what horse this was, for everyone in the city knew about Incitatus, but sometimes my mind doesn't

work very quickly, and especially when it comes up against the impossible.

'There is a rumour going round,' the slave boy said. 'Terrible news.'

He was panting hard and gasping out the words, and he had a strong English accent as well, so it wasn't easy for me to understand what he was saying.

'News?' I said.

'But it can't be true,' he said. 'I have to go and find out.'

'Find out what?' I said.

'Here,' he said, thrusting the golden chain into my hand. 'Take care of him. I'll find out the truth and come straight back.'

And before I could object he was gone, running down the street the way he had

come. The nerve of him! A slave, telling me what to do! I couldn't hold his horse for him, no matter how smartly it was dressed. I called out after him, but if he heard me he paid no attention. At the end of the street he hesitated and looked up and down. Then he slipped round the corner and was gone.

My brother needed the handcart to collect flour from the mill, and I had to get home. If I was late I would be in serious trouble. I had been out on my round since before dawn, and I needed to get something to eat and go to bed for a few hours, because my whole family had to work through the night to have fresh bread ready for the morning. On a good day, I got about five hours' sleep in the evening. On a good day, my mother and father got three.

It wasn't always like that. Life was a whole lot easier for all of us before the emperor Gaius took our horses and the best of our slaves. They say he sold the slaves and used the horses to transport Rome's treasures to Gaul so he could sell them, because he never had enough money for all his mad and extravagant projects.

I don't know if it's true, and I don't really
care. The end result was the same for us.
Our lives became one long, hard, circular
grind of baking and loading and delivering
and sleeping and getting up and baking
again. And I didn't have time to be standing
around holding horses, no matter how
glamorous they were.

And he really was glamorous. A racing
horse, I was sure, from the look of his
light bones and his fine, shiny coat. He
tossed his head and looked around him
with wild, fiery eyes, and he sniffed warily
at my empty cart as though he expected
it to jump up and bite him. You'd have
guessed by now, I'm sure, because everyone
– even people from out of town like

yourself – has heard about Emperor Gaius
and the things his madness caused him to
do, but I still hadn't worked out who it was
that I was taking care of.

While I was trying to
decide what to do, a man
came along the street – a
wealthy man, from the
shape of his belly
and the cut of his
toga. He stopped in front
of the horse and, to my
amazement, gave a bow.

'How nice to see
you out and about, Consul Incitatus,' he
said. 'Taking a little exercise, are you?
Getting to know your citizens?'

My knees went so weak that they would barely support me. This was absurd – it had to be a nightmare. It couldn't be happening.

'And you must be the consul's companion,' said the man, looking me up and down and making a clear effort to disguise his surprise and contempt. I'm a baker, after all. We have a tendency to be more than a little dusty.

I was rooted to the spot, my mind in turmoil. You see, the horse I was holding was a lot more than just a horse. After the emperor, the two consuls are Rome's most powerful officials, as I'm sure you know. If I was holding a dragon it couldn't have been more dangerous.

'Yes, sir,' I stammered. 'His companion.

Indeed. For today, that is.'

Our consuls are elected by the people, but this one was an exception. Emperor Gaius had flouted the Senate and made the decision himself. I found myself stroking the horse's neck, realized that this was no way to behave towards a consul, and stood to a kind of trembling attention. The rich man's eyes darkened.

'That is,' I spluttered, 'the consul is taking a stroll and I am accompanying him.'

I could tell that the man didn't believe a word I said, but what could he do? I saw a slim possibility of escape and leaped at it.

'Perhaps you would care to accompany him back to the palace yourself, sir?' I said, offering him the golden chain.

He backed away as though he had just noticed that I was a leper, and simpered something about very urgent business.

He bowed again to the horse, reversed a few steps in that position, then turned and scuttled away down the street as fast as his plump legs would carry him.

CHAPTER TWO

Under other circumstances I might
have found it funny to see that
man's undignified retreat. But I was in
far too much danger to laugh. If I was
caught, I was done for. You might think
that appointing a horse as your second in
command was a clever kind of joke, but
I can assure you there was nothing funny
about Emperor Gaius and his madness. We
had all celebrated when he took over as our
emperor. Anything had to be better than

Tiberius. That's what we thought, anyway.
It just goes to show how wrong you can be.

Littleboots, we called him, because he
used to wear miniature versions of soldiers'
boots when he was a child. Sounds so
innocent and affectionate, doesn't it? And
it was, to begin with. But by the time that
golden chain was put into my hand, the
mention of the name was enough to make
my blood run cold. He had become a
monster, a tyrant of the worst imaginable
kind.

I had to get out of there, and as soon as
I could persuade my legs to move I tried
to make a run for it. I dropped the chain,
picked up the handles of my cart and set
out for home. But the consul Incitatus had

other ideas. He had his own house beside
the palace, where important people went
to have dinner with him, and a retinue
of servants who looked after him night
and day. He wasn't used to being alone.
So when I went off down the street he
followed me, dragging the end of his
golden chain along the cobbles.

Alarmed as I was, I couldn't bring
myself to shout and wave my arms at one
of Rome's consuls, so there wasn't much I
could do to stop him. I put the handcart
down again and I was still trying to work
out what to do when I heard running
footsteps and turned to see a boy of about
my own age racing up behind me. There
was something about his urgency that
made me realize he wasn't on
any ordinary errand,
and I remembered
what the slave had
said about 'terrible
news'.

'What's up?' I
called to the boy.

He glanced at me as he raced past, but he didn't reply.

I looked back the way he had come. There was activity at the crossroads back there. I could see soldiers heading towards the palace and a flurry of people moving rapidly in the opposite direction. My innards began to churn in panic. I knew the city well, and I could read the signs. Something big was happening. And if Littleboots was behind it, as he was behind everything that happened in Rome, it meant that no one was safe.

My instinct was to bolt, but if I returned to the bakery without the cart I was going to find myself in a different kind of trouble. So I grabbed the handles again

and started trundling the stupid, clumsy
thing along the rutted street.

And still the consul Incitatus followed me.

There was a shout from behind. I turned
and saw the English slave who had left me
holding the horse. He was running down
the street towards me, but my initial sense
of relief didn't last longer than a heartbeat.
He was being pursued by a soldier, and the
soldier was winning.

'Save him!' the boy
yelled at me, and they
were the last words
he ever said, because at
that moment the soldier
caught him and ran him
through with his sword.

There were other soldiers in the street and they had seen me. It was impossible to miss me, in fact, with the horse's big purple blanket blazing out like a flag. There was only one way now for me to save my life, and I have to admit that I didn't stop to think about the consequences. They could be no worse than staying where I was. So I jumped from the ground to the handcart and from the handcart onto

Incitatus's purple-coated back, and I dug my heels into the consul's sides as hard as I possibly could.

CHAPTER THREE

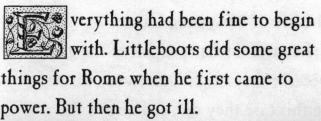

Everything had been fine to begin with. Littleboots did some great things for Rome when he first came to power. But then he got ill.

I was young at the time, but I still remember it well. My parents and grandparents paced the floor with worry. They joined the crowds at the temples, spending huge sums of money on sacrifices to the gods, pleading with them to spare the life of our young Caesar.

Be careful what you ask of the gods, because they might grant your wishes. In this case they did, and many's the person who has lived to regret the prayers and sacrifices they made at that time. Littleboots survived his illness, but most people will tell you that he never recovered from it. It changed him entirely. He began to say that he was a god, and he had the heads removed from all the statues

of Zeus and replaced with his own likeness. He spent all the money that was left in the treasury on crazy things like floating palaces, and then he came up with ways to take everyone else's money so he could keep on indulging himself.

My grandfather was one of his first victims. He was a respected figure in Rome and our bakery was the biggest and the best. So when Littleboots closed the granaries one day and wouldn't let out any grain for making bread, my grandfather went to see him to ask why. It wasn't only our business that would suffer. Without bread the people of Rome would be hungry.

Later that day my father and mother received an invitation to go to the palace for dinner. They always refused to tell me what happened, but my brother Lucius found out and he told me. My parents

were made to watch my grandfather being executed, and afterwards they had to sit and have dinner with Littleboots and pretend to make small talk and laugh at his jokes. And they did, because if they hadn't there was a good chance that their heads would have rolled like my grandfather's had, and what would have become of us children then?

If there is one thing to be thankful for, it is that my grandfather's death was relatively quick and painless. Since those days, Littleboots has become ingenious at finding new ways to kill people. The longer it takes and the more painful it is, the better he likes it. And that's why, when I got up on that horse's back, it wasn't for a lark. I was more frightened than I had ever been before. I was relying on the consul Incitatus to save my life.

CHAPTER FOUR

When I was small, before Littleboots took our carthorses, I was sometimes allowed to sit up on one of them while our good old slave, Drusus, led it on the delivery round. I never got to go faster than a shambling kind of trot, but I did at least know how it felt to have a horse underneath me. If I hadn't, I'm sure Incitatus would have lost me in the first three strides. He took off as though he was back on the racecourse; as if he was

sick and tired of being a consul and wanted
nothing more than a good gallop
around the streets.

    I clung on to his thick mane and prayed
to Artemis to keep me safe. The purple
blanket was no substitute for a saddle,
but it could have been worse. In the

summertime, so I'd heard, Incitatus wore
a silk one, and if he had been wearing that
now, my head would have been bouncing
off the cobbles.

I couldn't remember how to steer.
I'm not sure I ever learned, because the
carthorses always had someone leading
them. I wanted to turn to the right, but
the end of the chain was in my left hand
and on the left side of the horse's neck.
But if I pulled it and turned left, it would
lead me back towards the centre of the
city, straight into the swords of the palace
guard. The desire to stay alive gave me the
courage to do something that seemed, to
my inexperienced mind, to be practically
impossible. I leaned forward as far as I

could and passed the chain beneath the
horse's neck, from my left hand to my
right. Just in the nick of time I pulled
on it. The consul's head turned, and we
skidded round the corner and into the
next street.

Sparks flew from his shoes. Seeing
the open stretch of the street ahead of

him, Incitatus dropped his head and increased his speed. He swerved round a porter carrying a huge sack, who must have been deaf, because he didn't get out of the way. Everyone else in that street squeezed themselves flat against the walls as we went thundering by, the purple blanket fluttering like an empty sail behind us.

I changed hands again and turned Incitatus sharply to the left, into an alley that was too narrow for a cart. A girl flattened herself into a doorway. I saw the breeze of our passage ruffle her hair as we shot past. A smaller child squealed and called for its mother, and crouched beneath the open window of its house in terror.

Left again, not so sharply this time, and into another narrow street with tall apartment buildings leaning in to meet each other above our heads, and shutting out the light. They were badly built, most of those places, and several of them had collapsed over the past few years. Dozens of people had been killed, but there was no help for the survivors. Not from the builders or from the landlords or from the emperor. They could sleep on the streets for all anyone cared, and the truth is a lot of them did.

To the right again now, and then left, and straight on across another main thoroughfare. I prayed that it wouldn't be filled with soldiers looking for Incitatus.

It wasn't, but just as we got there our
crossing was blocked by two more of our
bakery handcarts, both of them empty.
One was being pushed by my brother,
Lucius, the other by my cousin, Quintus.
They heard the horse charging towards
them and abandoned the carts. Incitatus
hesitated, but he was going far too fast to
stop. He altered his stride and I felt his
decision through his body as he powered
forward and gathered himself for the
jump. I clung on, certain of disaster, but

the consul cleared the carts with ease and plunged straight on, into the opposite street.

One more right turn, then one more, and I was home. At the gates of our yard I hauled on the golden chain. The horse was reluctant to stop and we overshot the gates and went on several more yards before I got him under control and turned him back. I slid off and leaned, weak-kneed and quivering, against our compound gates.

CHAPTER FIVE

have a bit of a reputation in my family and it's not really fair. Whenever anything goes missing or gets broken, I get blamed for it whether it's my fault or not. It's true that I'm a bit on the clumsy side, and my arms and legs don't always go exactly where I want them to, but it's still not right to blame everything on me. I did lose two sacks of wheat once, but that was because a lad tricked me into going to look at an enormous fish, and while I was gone some other lads robbed my cart. And it's true that I once harnessed the wrong ox to the grinder. It was a young one that hadn't been properly trained, and it went berserk and pulled the whole thing to pieces. But everyone makes mistakes sometimes, don't they?

Wanted!

I'm not really a walking disaster, but I
have to admit I found myself wondering
about it as I hammered on the compound
gates. Maybe it would have been smarter
to keep riding until I reached the outskirts
of the city, and then abandon the horse
when he was too tired to follow me home.
But you know what? I couldn't have done
it. I was flushed with excitement after
the race through town, and I was totally
besotted with the horse that had shared the
adventure with me. He had looked after me,
done what I asked, and brought me safely
home. He had outrun the soldiers, kept
his feet on the uneven stones of the streets
and jumped a pair of handcarts. I wouldn't
have abandoned him now if Littleboots

himself had arrived to collect him.

Well. Maybe I would.

'Who is it?' my father called through the gates.

'It's me, Marcus,' I said. 'And ... and I've brought the consul Incitatus home with me.'

CHAPTER SIX

Incitatus and I stood in the middle
of the yard as the crowd around
us grew. First there was only my father,
staring at us as if we had dropped out of the
clouds, and then he was joined by my two
sisters, Tiberia and Appia, and my mother,
and then my aunt came out of her house
with two more of my cousins, and then my
grandmother and the two elderly slaves who
still looked after her.

None of them wanted to believe that it

was the consul Incitatus. My father wanted to strip all the finery off him and turn him out into the lane.

'Whatever he is, he's trouble,' he said. 'How could you be so stupid as to bring him here?'

I told the story again, carefully explaining that I'd had no choice, but no one seemed to understand.

'Better to keep the horse and throw the boy out,' said my aunt. 'He's nothing but trouble and always has been.'

I saw my mother turn on her and braced myself for another of their interminable rows, but just then Incitatus raised his tail and dropped a heap of steaming manure on to the dusty floor of the yard. That silenced everyone. Not because of the smell and the mess. We have always had animals in the yard – horses in the old days; only oxen now. It was what we saw in the dung that left us all speechless. It glittered. It shone. It was full of tiny sparkling pieces of gold.

That was another of the stories that everyone had heard about the emperor's favourite horse but no one ever quite believed. Incitatus was fed on mangoes and apples, and on oats mixed through with gold flake.

My aunt looked around. With the gates closed no one could see into our compound, but all the same it was as though there were eyes everywhere. We all felt it. My older sister, Appia, scooped the dung into a bucket and hid it underneath the lemon tree.

'We have to get him out of sight,' my mother said. She opened the door to one of the stables and let our three dogs out.

Two of the other stables had broken roofs and the remaining ones had gradually filled up with junk since the horses had gone.

I led Incitatus to the door. He stopped.

'Come on,' I said. 'Nice stable for you, see?'

But the consul did not agree, and refused to go in. My father raised his arms and growled at him, but Incitatus laid back his ears and ignored him.

'Get him in!' said my aunt, and we could all hear the panic in her voice. 'Quickly! Before someone comes and sees him.'

Appia fetched the whip we use to drive the oxen on the grinder, and my father raised it threateningly, but Incitatus took exception to this and reversed determinedly away from the stable door, dragging me helplessly with him.

'Stupid boy!' said my aunt, but neither she nor my father dared actually use the whip on Incitatus. Horse or no horse, he was one of Rome's consuls and a member of the emperor's household.

'At least take off the purple robe,' said my mother.

But no one dared to do that, either, and while we were all standing around wondering what to do next, there was a loud knock at the yard gates.

The dogs barked. Everyone froze where they stood, with the exception of Incitatus, who gave me a hard nudge with his nose and began to walk over to the inviting double doors of the bakery. I pulled him up, but my mother shook her head and

gestured to me to take him in there. This time he didn't hesitate but marched

straight into the dark, sweet-scented
building. I can't say I blamed him. It was
a palace compared with that small, doggy
stable. My mother closed the door behind
us and I heard my father quieten the dogs
and ask who was at the gates.

'Quintus and Lucius,' came my brother's
voice. 'Let us in, quick!'

Even behind the bakery doors I could
hear the monstrous sigh as everyone let out
their breath together. The gates creaked
and the handcarts rattled in. I knocked.
My mother opened the doors a crack and
let me out.

'Have you heard the news?' Lucius was
saying.

'What news?' said my father.

But my brother waited until the gates were firmly closed and bolted and the family gathered in a close huddle around him before he would say any more. Even then he whispered as he told us what he had heard.

'It isn't certain,' he said, 'but they're saying on the street that Littleboots is dead.'

CHAPTER SEVEN

You would expect us to celebrate, perhaps, to clap and cheer and dance around the compound with delight. We didn't. Instead a silence fell over us, so profound that even the dogs stopped their energetic activities and slumped down in the dust. Behind the bakery doors, Incitatus whickered anxiously, and I heard the thud-thud-thud of more of his golden droppings landing on the spotless floor. Every one of us hoped that what we had heard was true, but every one of us, from my aged grandmother right down to my seven-year-old cousin, was thinking the same thing.

It was a trick.

It would be just like Littleboots to do something like that. Spread the word that he was dead and then, while people were celebrating and sacrificing victims to the gods, send out his soldiers to arrest them all for disloyalty. Then he could confiscate their property and use the proceeds to finance his vile appetites, and send them to the Circus Maximus to fight his professional gladiators, or cut off their hands and string them round their necks, or feed them to his lions

and alligators and other dreadful beasts.

But we would not fall into that trap. We stayed silent. Incitatus whickered again and I opened one of the doors so he could see us.

'We continue as usual,' said my grandmother at last. She spoke softly,

afraid of eavesdroppers. 'We do nothing
and say nothing until we smell the smoke
from his funeral pyre.'

'Not even then,' said my father. 'I would
need more proof than that.'

'Who will be emperor next?' said my
little sister, Tiberia.

'Shh,' said my mother. 'Hold your
tongue.'

We had a plan then, about how to react
to the rumour. But we still had a serious
problem on our hands.

'What are we going to do about the
consul?' I said.

'The best plan,' said my father, 'is to wait
until dark, then strip all the finery off him
and turn him out on to the street.'

'That kind of plan never works,' said my mother. 'There's always some child or a nosy old sweeper who's bound to see you. And what would it look like, turning loose a perfectly good horse?'

My grandmother agreed. 'He'd have us in our own ovens if he ever found out we did that.'

'In any case,' I said, 'he likes us. If we turned him out he wouldn't go anywhere. He'd just stand outside the gates until we let him back in.'

My aunt glared at me, but she didn't say anything.

'So there's two choices, as far as I can see,' said my mother. 'We take him back to the palace and hand him over, or we keep

him here, hidden away, until we discover
what has happened.'

'There's another thing we can do,' said
hard man Quintus. 'We can cut him up and
feed him to the dogs.'

Lucius grinned. 'That would serve
Littleboots right.'

My grandmother stepped forward into
our midst. 'Now listen, all of you,' she
said. 'That boy' – she poked me hard in
the collarbone – 'came riding in here this
afternoon at a very high speed. The horse
is wearing a purple robe and a head collar
dripping with jewels. Does everyone
here really believe that no one will have
noticed?'

Everyone didn't. When we stopped to

think about it, no one did.

'Someone, somewhere, knows that Incitatus is here,' my grandmother went on. 'So losing him or feeding him to the dogs will do us no good.'

Quintus shrugged, but everyone else nodded, and my grandmother continued: 'It's my opinion that your son, my own grandson, signed a death sentence for everyone in this family when he brought Incitatus to these gates.'

My heart stopped and my breath got stuck in my throat. I felt as though I was already standing in front of Littleboots, waiting to hear what particular horrors he had chosen for me.

'No!' I managed to blurt.

'He didn't mean it,' said my mother, moving closer to me.

'Always the same,' said my grandmother. 'Never stops to think.'

'Well, what would you have done in his position?' asked my mother indignantly.

'What I would have done is beside the point,' said my grandmother. 'It's what we do now that will decide whether we live or die.'

'And that is ... ?' said my father.

'We treat the consul as an honoured guest. You invite him into your house and give him the best bedroom.'

'My house!' said my father. 'Why not your house?'

'Because mine is humble and small and

yours is large and elegant. Or at least, it used to be when I lived in it.'

He had to concede the point. 'And what then?' he said. 'What happens if they discover him here?'

'Then we tell the truth. We say that we heard dreadful rumours concerning the health of the emperor, and your son witnessed unrest and violence not far from the palace. For the consul's own safety he invited him to reside with us until the situation settled down and the true facts became known.'

'I invited him?' I said.

'Indeed you did,' said my grandmother. 'And he most graciously accepted.'

CHAPTER EIGHT

I didn't sleep much that night. I doubt whether anyone in our compound did, but I slept least of all. We had tried to leave the consul Incitatus alone, once we had covered the floor of our guest bedroom with fresh straw and given him as much hay and oats as our bullocks would eat in a week. But he wasn't used to being on his own and he wouldn't settle. Needless to say, I was the one who was sent in to keep him company.

And I was very comfortable, actually. The bed in that room had been built in there and wouldn't fit out of the door, so we had pushed it against the wall to make room for the horse. I unrolled my own mattress on it and I was as comfortable as I would have been anywhere. So it wasn't discomfort that kept me awake.

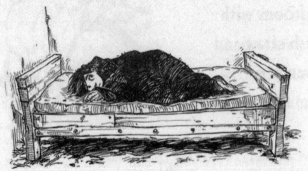

It was fear. Fear that Incitatus would be
discovered and that Littleboots wouldn't
accept our excuses. My head filled with
florid imaginings, and I dredged up all the
memories I had of the ways Littleboots
had invented for putting people to
death. They went from bad to worse to
unthinkable. I wondered whether anyone
had ever been given a choice, and which
method I would pick, if I had to.

But I did finally get to sleep, and it was
Incitatus himself who helped me. He came
close to the bedside and lay down there
on the floor, and the regular swell of his
breathing began to lull me. I had to admit
that he was nice company, the consul, and I
couldn't imagine any other member of the

Roman Senate being so quiet and gentle.

'Perhaps you'll be the next Caesar,' I whispered into his ear.

And, imagining that, I finally slipped into sleep.

CHAPTER NINE

For the first time in as long as I can remember my mother didn't get me up in the middle of the night to help with the bread making. I woke to the sound of the handcarts in the yard, and the creak of the compound gates as they opened. Incitatus was already up and nosing around in the marble basin where we'd put his oats the day before. There were fresh droppings in the straw, but you had to look very hard to see any gold in them now, because most of it had already passed through his system.

I got up and fetched him more oats, then drew water and filled up his trough. He made a big show of splashing at the water with his nose before he drank it, and I wondered whether he was used to having it warmed for him, or whether we were insulting him and ought to be giving him wine instead. But he blew sweet breath into my face and stood quite contentedly

as I groomed his mane with my mother's

 comb and polished his coat with her best silk shawl. I liked it very much, this job. It was better than delivering bread any day.

My mother brought me breakfast, and some fruit for Incitatus, and afterwards, because there was nothing left to do, I climbed back into bed and went to sleep again. I dreamed that I was riding into battle alongside Littleboots's father, the

mighty Germanicus, but I got left behind
because my horse was lame. When I looked
down I saw its hind legs were missing,
and Littleboots was crouching beside me,
roasting them over an open fire.

That afternoon, when everyone had
returned from the deliveries, we had
another family gathering in the yard.

Wanted!

The streets were full of rumours and
speculation, and it was impossible to
know what was true. Lucius had heard that
Littleboots was murdered by members
of the praetorian guard, and that they
killed his wife and baby daughter as well,
but since the praetorian guard is there to
look after the emperor's personal safety,
it seemed impossible to us. Other people
were saying that the whole thing was a
trick, as we had feared, and that there were
public executions taking place beside the
palace and that the streets were running
with blood. This couldn't be confirmed
because no one had the courage to go
anywhere near there, and the streets
surrounding the palace were unusually

quiet and empty. My father had heard that Littleboots's body had been taken to a private garden and they had tried to cremate it, but there hadn't been enough wood for a proper pyre and they'd had to bury what was left of him. And someone else told my cousin that rioters had overrun the forum and that there was no longer any kind of government in the city.

But the maddest rumour of all, the one that cheered us all up and gave us a good laugh, was that there were plans afoot to crown Claudius as the next Caesar. He was Littleboots's uncle and the only member of his family who had escaped death or banishment. It was said, and it was probably true, that Littleboots only spared his life because he enjoyed making fun of him in public. People liked him, on the whole, poor, daft, stammering old Claudius, but the idea of him becoming emperor was ridiculous.

So we decided, at our gathering, to believe the worst and ignore the best and, for the meantime at least, to carry on as we were and to stick to the agreed story. The consul Incitatus was our honoured guest and we were caring for him until Rome settled down.

But that night, well after dark, a neighbour called at our gates and she had new information. She had heard that soldiers were going from door to door throughout the city and were searching all the outbuildings. Several horses had been confiscated and their owners dragged off along with them. No one could say why. Our neighbour was aware, she said, that we had no horses now, but there was no harm in passing on the news, all the same.

She did know, of course. As my grandmother had said, it would have been impossible for me to come galloping into our little back lane without someone in the neighbourhood noticing. But she had been a loyal friend by tipping us off, and in dangerous times like ours there aren't so many of them left. We were lucky. Very lucky indeed.

CHAPTER TEN

t was my little sister Tiberia who ran into the guest room to tell me what the neighbour had said about the

soldiers and the searches. Before I could get my head around it, Lucius stormed in, with the rest of the family at his heels.

'We have to get him out of here,' he said.
'And quickly, before the soldiers arrive and
drag us all off to our deaths.'

He pushed me aside and began to yank
at the buckle at the front of the purple
blanket. The consul took exception to
this, and laid his ears back and began to
reverse across the room, but it was my
grandmother who stopped my brother
from going any further.

'No,' she said, and her voice carried all
the authority of her seventy years. 'I will
not allow anything to be done in a state
of panic. You may be right, Lucius, but
we have to think this through and reach a
proper decision.'

Lucius was red in the face with rage, but

my grandmother's word was law and he didn't dare act against her. I thought I was off the hook but now the full force of her authority was turned upon me.

'You, boy!' she said. 'You will clean up this mess and put fresh straw down. Then you will polish that . . . that consul until every hair of his coat shines like gold. If they find Incitatus in here they must have no complaints about the way he has been looked after.'

I ran to get a basket to collect the dung. When I came back, the rest of the family were moving off towards the front of the house to continue their discussions. For the moment at least, the bread making was forgotten.

I gathered the droppings
and the wet straw and
went to get some fresh
stuff. The compound
was unusually quiet,
with everyone at the
meeting inside my
parents' house, and
as I was carrying the straw
across it I suddenly knew that it was up
to me to sort out this problem, and that
I would have to do it alone. And I knew
exactly how I would have to do it.

You might think it was brave of me,
but it wasn't really. Not when you stop
to think about it. The way we saw it,
Littleboots had sent out his soldiers to

find his favourite horse; his best friend and trusted consul. Already people were being arrested because he was missing and they didn't even have Incitatus. We did.

Of course, it was possible that the emperor and his soldiers would be delighted that we had invited the consul into our home and taken such care of him. Littleboots might give us back our horses and shower honours upon the whole family. But despite what my grandmother said, I just couldn't see it happening. As I crossed the yard I had a vision of it running with blood, and littered with teeth and fingers and ears. 'Put him to death so he knows he is dying.' That was one of Littleboots's milder declarations. He insisted on his victims suffering for as long as possible. Some of them took days to die. There were stories I had heard that were too dreadful to think about.

So the question I was left with was a simple one. All of us, or just one? And the answer to that was obvious. Just one.

But which one?

Simple again. The one who'd caused the problem in the first place.

CHAPTER ELEVEN

They were all talking so quietly that I couldn't hear a thing when I went into the house. The consul was pleased to see me back, and his ears pricked with excitement when I gathered up the golden chain and attached it to his head collar. As I opened the guest-room door a sudden image flashed into my mind of the statue of Jupiter in the Capitol, his head replaced by Littleboots's, his thunderbolt raised, ready to strike. The vision stopped

79

me in my tracks and made my innards
churn, but it didn't shake my resolve. I
took a deep breath and led Incitatus out
into the yard, then through the compound
gates into the street.

There was practically no one about,
and those there were kept a low profile:
hooded ghosts vanishing into black
corners. What I did see, though, was
horses. In practically every street there
was a cob or a carthorse or a child's riding
pony, each one of them turned out from
its warm stable to save its owner from
arrest. And the saddest thing of all was
that not one of those beasts could possibly
have been mistaken for Incitatus. It was
yet another example of the terror that

Littleboots created with every order he gave.

I had no clear idea of what I was doing, beyond getting Incitatus as far from my family compound as possible before I abandoned him. When I think of it now I see that I ought to have stripped him of his finery before I left home, and put the blanket and the bejewelled head collar under one of the bread ovens to burn.

I ought to have chased him away down one
of those dark streets and run off before he
could find me and follow me. But a strange
thing began to happen, and I became
fascinated by it, and instead of getting
away from Incitatus I clambered up on to
his back. The abandoned horses began to
follow us. First one, then another, and
then a couple more that had already joined
up together. If Incitatus minded he didn't

show it. He walked with long, graceful strides, his head high, gazing around at the dim streets of Rome as though he knew that he was second in command only to the emperor, and that the place as good as belonged to him.

And still I stayed on board, taken in by the consul's confidence, seduced by the little procession of horses into a dream of power. When I look back on it now I see that I wasn't in my right mind that night. I was puffed up with pride at my own heroism and filled with sweet anguish by my noble gesture of self-sacrifice. I became Germanicus, Rome's greatest hero, returning triumphant from my latest campaign. More horses joined us; my army following along behind. The rejoicing crowds parted before us. I never fathered that monster, Littleboots, but I became emperor myself instead, and I was the kindest, most generous Caesar the empire had ever known.

And then, too suddenly, there were real soldiers there. There were about eight of them, and they were all asleep at the side of the street. I hauled on the chain, but

there was no stopping Incitatus now. He shook his head and jerked on the rein and just kept going. The sounds of all those horses woke the soldiers and they jumped up in confusion, shouting orders to each other. I still could have escaped if I'd had my wits about me. It took them ages to get a torch alight, and even when they finally succeeded and saw Incitatus in his fine attire, they didn't seem to know how to react. If I had slipped off and scarpered I would have been miles away before they got themselves organized, and they could never have found me in the dark. But by the time I thought about it I was surrounded, and it was far too late.

The soldiers stood around and looked

at the consul, and one or two of them gave
little bows, and the others looked at them
and they looked back at the others, but
during that whole awkward comedy

I don't remember any of them looking up at me. Finally the leader of the little troop cleared his throat.

'Consul Incitatus,' he said. 'We are very glad to have found you at last. Your presence is requested at the Capitol.'

CHAPTER TWELVE

Those soldiers hadn't a clue what to do with me, so they ignored me entirely, as though I was the consul's little dog that he had been taking for a walk. They didn't know what to do about the other horses either, so they just let them come along too, even though some of them started getting excited and trotting on ahead, so the whole procession became a bewildering muddle of soldiers and horses, with Incitatus and me strolling along in the middle.

I was very frightened now that I had come out of my daydream, but I had missed my chance to run. I could only hope that I remained as invisible as I appeared to be, and that I might find another moment to escape later on. For a long time we walked through the dark streets, and if anyone was awake at that hour in Rome they were very careful not to let the soldiers know it. There wasn't a lamp or a candle to be seen anywhere, and our only light was cast by the single guttering torch somewhere near the head of the procession. But when we turned into the forum there was suddenly light everywhere. And people, gathered around the temples and the streets between them.

They weren't in a big crowd but in small
groups here and there, some standing, some
sitting, some wrapped in blankets and
sleeping.

We marched through them, and I saw
eyes, one pair after another, turned towards

us in weary bewilderment. And then someone spotted Incitatus, and the whole sleepy gathering suddenly came alive.

'The consul!' a woman shouted, and the news was taken up and bounced along the street.

'The consul is here!'

'Incitatus is found!'

'Consul Incitatus is on his way!'

I swear the horse understood. He arched his beautiful neck and lifted his feet high, dancing on his toes with all

the raw energy of the racehorse in him and
with all the haughty dignity of a Roman
consul. We were surrounded by light now
as people closed in around us with their
lamps and torches to get a better look. As
we left the forum and began to climb the
steep path up the Capitoline Hill, loose
horses thundered through the patches of
darkness beyond, kicking up their heels in
excitement and tearing back to rejoin the
throng.

Someone blew a long note on a horn.
The soldiers, wide awake now and
extremely proud of themselves, waved
cheerfully at the onlookers. There were
more people waiting at the top of the
hill, and when we reached it a cheer went

up. With a sudden rush of exhilaration,
I realized that something had changed. I
wasn't sure why, but I knew that this city
no longer felt like Littleboots's Rome.

CHAPTER THIRTEEN

News ran ahead of us, so by the time Incitatus and I arrived at the doors of the Capitol the senators who had been dozing inside were awake and on their feet. When I saw them in their robes of office I realized that this was no place for me, and I chose that moment to jump off. I could easily

have slipped away and vanished into the
night, but I'd done a stupid thing. I had
wrapped the end of the
chain around my hand as
we walked through the
streets of Rome, and now
I couldn't unwind it.

Incitatus didn't hesitate for
an instant. He strode right in as though
he owned the place, and the pressure of
soldiers and onlookers behind us pushed
me along with him, still attached to
the golden chain. Behind us the doors
closed, shutting the loose horses and the
onlookers outside. The soldiers stayed
at the doors, acting as guards now, and
Incitatus and I were on our own.

As though he knew exactly where he
was going, he strode down the aisle
that the standing senators had created. I
managed to get my hand free of the chain,
but it was too late now for me to get away.
I glanced down at myself, suddenly aware
that I had been wearing the same grubby
tunic for a fortnight and that my feet,
where they showed through my sandals,
were as black as charcoal. But I don't think
anyone else noticed. I watched the faces as
we passed. Every last eye was fixed upon
the horse, and not a single one fell upon
me. I was, to my relief, still invisible.

We were heading straight for the central
point of the Capitol, where the statue of
Jupiter, with Littleboots's head, always

stood. But Jupiter/Littleboots was gone. In its place was a very small statue on a very tall pedestal. It wasn't grand, but it was Jupiter, and it bore no resemblance whatsoever to our corrupt emperor. I was still gazing at it, trying to take in the significance of it, when our course was altered by a curve in the wall of senators, and after another few steps we came to a halt in front of a man in the fine robes of a consul. Behind him, surrounded by members of the praetorian guard, was an old man sitting in a heavy wooden chair. His chin had dropped on to his chest and he was fast asleep, but I recognized him all the same. Everyone in Rome knew that face. It was Littleboots's daft old uncle, Claudius.

CHAPTER FOURTEEN

The other consul cleared his throat and spoke above the murmur of voices in the Capitol.

'Now that Consul Incitatus is here we can continue with the proceedings in hand,' he said.

The senators broke up their makeshift corridor and took seats in a semicircle around the other consul and Claudius, who was still asleep and gently snoring. I realized that Incitatus was standing with

his back to them all and, as unobtrusively
as I could, I prodded him in the side
until he turned
round. This,
unfortunately,
brought me
to a position
right beside
the other
consul, and he
stared at me as if
I was a bad smell,
which I quite
possibly was. He
opened his mouth as if he was going to
speak to me, then thought better of it and
turned his attention to the assembly.

'It is the unanimous decision of the senators here gathered that, following the death of Gaius Caesar Augustus Germanicus, his uncle Claudius be immediately crowned the new Caesar.'

It was true then, that rumour that had gone around. But I still couldn't believe my ears. Claudius? Emperor of Rome? It had to be some kind of joke.

To my right there was a mild kerfuffle as efforts were made to wake up the old man.

'W-w-w-what?' he stammered.

'I presume,' the consul went on, 'that this decision meets with the approval of Incitatus?'

Once again all heads turned in my

direction, but once again not one eye alighted on me. The horse stood proudly, soaking up all the attention, but perfectly still. He made no gesture that could be taken as either approval or dissent. He didn't even blink.

I suddenly understood why it had been so important that Incitatus be found. The consent of both consuls was needed before a new emperor could be instated. Incitatus might be a horse, but he was still a consul, and without his approval Claudius could not officially be made Caesar.

Still the assembly waited. Something had to be done. I put out my hand, fingers closed, beneath Incitatus's muzzle and, thinking I had a treat for him, he dipped

his head. Finding I had nothing, he lifted
it again. It was all that was needed. A cheer
went through the assembly and Claudius
was helped to his feet. The other consul
put a purple robe around his shoulders and
a laurel wreath on his head. There were
more cheers, uproarious ones, and I heard
them spread beyond the Capitol and into

the square outside. I knew that soon the streets would be full of runners, carrying the wonderful news across the city and gathering the masses to come and pay their respects to the new Caesar. I couldn't wait to see my family and tell them that I was here in the Capitol to see old Claudius crowned.

But the proceedings here were not yet over. The other consul took centre stage again and called for quiet. When at last he got it, he said, 'I would like to suggest that, as Claudius Caesar's first act in office, he remove the travesty that is the shame of the Roman Empire and relieve Incitatus of the consulship.'

There was a burst of enthusiastic

agreement, and Claudius was led forward
to perform his first duty.

'Y-y-y-yes,' he said. 'I agree. N-n-nice
horse b-b-but not a c—, a c—, not a consul.
Not any l-l-longer, anyway.'

Like hounds on a fallen stag a pack of
senators descended upon poor Incitatus
and ripped off his purple blanket and his
beautiful head collar. The horse shrank
away from the pulling and dragging hands,
but there was nowhere for him to go
and he had to submit. Yet again I was
ignored, but when the horse had been
stripped of all his finery, someone did
think to push a piece of coarse rope into
my hand. I put it around Incitatus's neck
and his nose and made a rough halter.

'Who do you appoint in his place, Caesar?' said the remaining consul.

'Oh. Oh, yes,' said Claudius. 'Wh-wh-who indeed?'

He looked around in bewilderment, and someone in the front row of seats seized  the opportunity to leap to his feet and stick his hand up.

'Yes,' said Claudius, 'y-y-you'll do, whatever your name is. T-t-temporarily. Until the n-n-next election.'

There was another huge cheer. Someone tossed the horse's purple blanket at the newly appointed consul and the entire assembly collapsed into fits of laughter. When order was finally restored, the new appointee, now dressed in proper consular garb, came forward and called for quiet.

'I have a suggestion for your second official pronouncement,' he said. 'I propose that you offer this horse, this sorry reminder of your nephew's reign, to the great god Jupiter. He has been offended by the madness of Littleboots, and Rome must make amends. What better way of doing that than to offer him the horse as a blood sacrifice?'

CHAPTER FIFTEEN

o!' I screamed. 'No, no, no, no, no!"

But my cries were drowned out by the din of a hundred approving voices. Already senators were moving forward to take hold of Incitatus and bring him to the place of sacrifice, but there was another voice as well as mine, clamouring to be heard above the mob.

'S-s-s-stop it! I c-c-command you to s-s-stop this n-n-now!'

Claudius was standing up and waving his arms around, but it was some time before he was noticed, and order was called, and the frenzied racket died down.

'I know why you have been so k-k-keen to ap-ap-appoint me your new emperor,' said Claudius. 'You all think you can w-w-w-walk all over me and m-m-make me do what you w-w-want. But this is what I w-w-want. This b-b-b-boy here has something to s-s-say. L-l-let him he heard.'

And he turned and looked at me. And both the consuls looked as me as well, and all the senators.

I wasn't invisible any longer. The emperor himself had made me real; a human being with an opinion and a right to be heard. Tears erupted without warning and streamed down my face. I felt dirty and smelly and very, very small, but I had to speak up. It wasn't for me, you see. It was for Incitatus.

'Don't kill him,' I said. 'Please don't kill him. He didn't ask to be made into a consul. He couldn't help any of it. He's only a horse.'

And he was. He knew, you see. I swear he did. Without his purple blanket and his fancy head collar he was just an old racehorse who had had his day. His head drooped as if he was ashamed. The proud spark had completely vanished from his eye.

And seeing him like that gave me an idea.

'Perhaps you should start your reign in a different way,' I said, and I was so glad that it was old Claudius I was speaking to, because I could never have spoken to anyone else in authority that way. 'Perhaps you should begin with an act of generosity instead of an act of violence.'

There were murmurs of disapproval from the assembly but Claudius held up his hand.

'G-g-go on,' he said.

'I'm the son of a baker, sir,' I said. 'And your nephew, the emperor Gaius, he took all our horses away and left us with nothing to pull our carts. Give us this horse in return, sir. As a replacement for the ones he took.'

Wanted!

There was more disapproval from the senators, but Claudius was grinning with delight.

'Yes,' he said. 'T-t-take him, boy, and let him deliver b-b-b-bread to the p-p-people of Rome. I can think of no better way for the consul Incitatus to end his days.'

CHAPTER SIXTEEN

And there he is now, as you can see. He has been pulling a bread cart for us ever since, day in and day out. And

do you know what? He loves it – don't you, Incy? Never gets tired of it. Never puts a foot wrong. Willing and good-tempered whatever the hour and whatever the weather.

The thing is, all the dreadful things you heard about Littleboots are true. He was a monster, there's no two ways about it. I will never understand what made him do such terrible things, but I do understand one thing about him. I know why he loved this horse. There was never an animal like him, was there, Incy? See him there? Understands every word I say, don't you, boy?

But I can't stay here chatting all day. My bread's going stale. I'll tell you one last thing about this horse, though. If I was made emperor tomorrow, this lad would be made consul the day after that.

And the other one? I don't know who I'd pick. I've got a very clever little dog at home. People are strange creatures, in my opinion. You can never really trust them. They might start out well enough, but power always gets the better of them in the end. Mind you, it hasn't got the better of old Claudius yet, has it? Smart guy, that, pretending to be a fool and keeping his nephew sweet.

Not such a duffer though, is he? Best Caesar Rome ever had, if you ask me. Look, Incy agrees with me, don't you, Incy? He knows what a narrow escape he had. Long live the emperor Claudius, that's what I say. And if Incy could speak, that's exactly what he'd say too.

AUTHOR'S NOTE

Littleboots is based upon Caligula, who was emperor of Rome between AD 37 and 41. The background details in the story are based upon my research into his rule, but I have taken some liberties as well. He did have a favourite racehorse called Incitatus, and the horse did have its own living quarters and servants. But although Caligula threatened to make Incitatus a consul, he didn't actually do it.